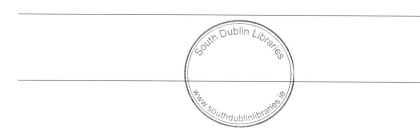

This Little Tiger book belongs to:

The Bartletts' Bathroom

PING'S
POWDER ROOM

WENDY'S W.C.

NELLIE'S
POTTY

BUDDY'S
BOG

COLIN'S
CAN

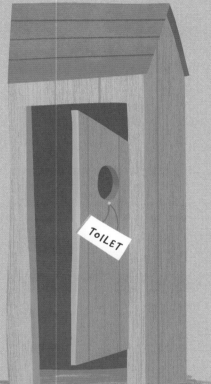

For my brother, Craig
(and all the times we shared
the queue for the toilet!)
~ K N

For Heather and Rob
~ D B

The Forest Stewardship Council® (FSC®) is an international,
non-governmental organisation dedicated to promoting responsible
management of the world's forests. FSC® operates a system of forest
certification and product labelling that allows consumers to identify
wood and wood-based products from well-managed forests.

For more information about the FSC®, please visit their website at www.fsc.org

LITTLE TIGER PRESS LTD,
an imprint of the Little Tiger Group
1 Coda Studios, 189 Munster Road, London SW6 6AW
Imported into the EEA by Penguin Random House Ireland,
Morrison Chambers, 32 Nassau Street, Dublin D02 YH68
www.littletiger.co.uk

First published in Great Britain 2020

Printed in China
LTP/2800/4603/0422

10 9 8 7 6

I REALLY REALLY NEED A WEE

KARL NEWSON

DUNCAN BEEDIE

LiTTLE TiGER

LONDON

Uh-oh!

I really, really, really, really,
REALLY NEED A WEE!

I need a wee so desperately
- I'm jiggly! *Can't you see?!*

I wasn't desperate back at home,
but now I am out here . . .

I really, really need a wee.

Oh dear. Oh dear.

OH DEAR!

I need to think of something else
to make the feeling go . . .

a waterfall!

Oh no.

Oh no.

OH NO!

I have to find a toilet – **QUICK!**
I'm desperate as can be!

I really, really, really, really,
REALLY NEED A WEE!

Aha!
A hole to duck
into . . .

But – **WHOOPS!** – a mouse lives there!

At **last!**
A bush to go behind . . .

Argh! **Someone** beat me to it!
(I really should have knocked first,
but there wasn't time to do it.)

And now I've got to run because
a bear is chasing me . . .

And I still really,

really, really,

REALLY

NEED A WEE!

Hmm . . . maybe I can lose the bear
by climbing really high?
There isn't room for both of us!

Uh-oh.

Oh dear!

Goodbye!

Sorry, Bear.
I really am!
I hope that you can see . . .

I'm jiggly-wiggly-

wobbly-wibbly

BURSTING

for a wee!

YES! At last – a toilet!
But OH **NO!**

TOILET

Look at
the queue!

A **HUNDRED** others just like me
who need the bathroom too!

Woohoo!

What a **feeling!**
What relief!
I'm **jiggly-wiggly** free!

From now on
I'll think twice
about how much
I need a wee.

Look at all those silly monkeys
lined up in the queue!

Oh dear!

Oh no!

A BIG uh-oh!

I think I need . . .

a
poo!

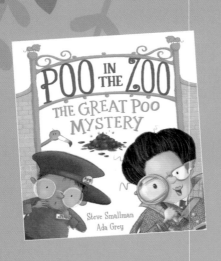

POO IN THE ZOO

THE GREAT POO MYSTERY

Steve Smallman
Ada Grey

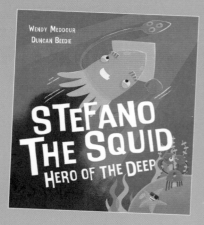

WENDY MEDDOUR
DUNCAN BEEDIE

STEFANO THE SQUID

HERO OF THE DEEP

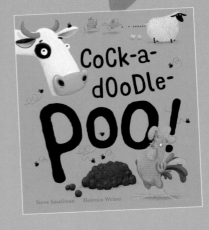

CoCk-a-dOoDle-PoO!

Steve Smallman   Florence Weiser

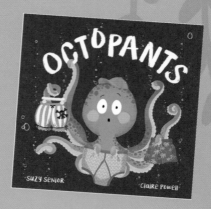

OCTOPANTS

SUZY SENIOR   CLAIRE POWELL

Woohoo! More hilarious books from Little Tiger . . .

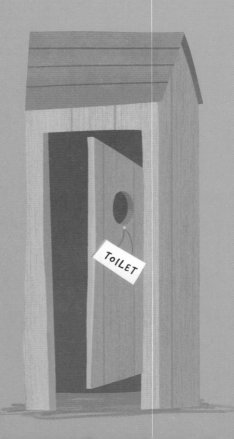

ToILET

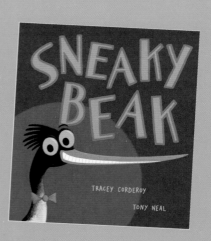

SNEAKY BEAK

TRACEY CORDEROY

TONY NEAL

NOW YOU SEE ME NOW YOU DON'T

Patricia Hegarty   Jonny Lambert

LITTLE TIGER

For information regarding any of the above titles or for our catalogue, please contact us: Little Tiger Press Ltd, 1 Coda Studios, 189 Munster Road, London SW6 6AW • Tel: 020 7385 6333
E-mail: contact@littletiger.co.uk • www.littletiger.co.uk